THE DAY MY BROTHER MARTIN CHANGED THE WORLD

by CHRISTINE KING FARRIS    *Illustrated by* LONDON LADD

SCHOLASTIC PRESS / NEW YORK

# ACKNOWLEDGMENTS

The great March on Washington was indeed a signature event in the history

and life of our country. I am pleased to share my knowledge and thoughts about it with the

younger generation.Thanks to Denene Millner and London Ladd for their invaluable assistance

in the presentation of this momentous event. My thanks also to editor Andrea Pinkney

and Scholastic for making this book available to young readers.

—CHRISTINE KING FARRIS

Text copyright © 2008 by Christine King Farris
Illustrations copyright © 2008 by London Ladd

Library of Congress Cataloging-in-Publication Data

Farris, Christine King.
March on! : the day my brother Martin changed the world / Christine King Farris ; illustrated by London Ladd.  1st ed.
p. cm.
ISBN-13: 978-0-545-03537-8
ISBN-10: 0-545-03537-6
1. King, Martin Luther, Jr., 1929–1968. I have a dream—Juvenile literature. 2. King, Martin Luther, Jr., 1929–1968 Oratory — Juvenile literature. 3. Speeches, addresses, etc., American — Washington (D.C.) — Juvenile literature. 4. March on Washington for Jobs and Freedom, Washington, D.C., 1963 — Juvenile literature. 5. Civil rights demonstrations — Washington (D.C.) — History 20th century — Juvenile literature. 6.  Farris, Christine King — Juvenile literature. 7. King, Martin Luther, Jr., 1929–1968 — Family — Juvenile literature. 8. African Americans — Civil rights History — 20th century — Juvenile literature.  I. Ladd, London, ill. II. Title.

E185.97.K5F369 2008
323.092 — dc22
[B]
2007038620

Printed in Singapore  46

10 9 8 7 6 5 4 3 2 1
First edition, September 2008
The text type was set in 12 point ITC Bookman Light.
Book design by Susan Schultz

*This book is dedicated to my granddaughter Farris Christine Watkins and others of her generation who must continue to espouse and carry forth the message delivered by my brother Martin Luther King Jr. on that eventful and great day.*
—Christine King Farris

*To three special ladies — Victoria, Theresa, and Lavanda, whose love and support make it possible to do what I love.*
—London Ladd

**M**y brother Martin never bragged. Martin was always very modest. When we were growing up, Mother Dear and Daddy taught all of us—Martin, our little brother, Alfred Daniel, and me, Christine—to do good for others. They told us not to be "chesty" about doing right. "Don't go sticking out your chest, all puffed up and proud," Mother Dear often said. "Chesty is not the way to be."

So, even though Martin got a load of attention for protesting and for speaking out, he couldn't have imagined how many people would come to the great March on Washington for Jobs and Freedom in 1963.

**BUT COME THEY DID.** From northern cities like Detroit and Chicago. From southern cities such as Birmingham, Atlanta, and Memphis. They came from small towns, too. From places such as Danville, Virginia, and Albany, Georgia, and Orangeburg, South Carolina.

Some of them rode the bus. Others came on the train. A bunch walked all the way from Brooklyn, more than 230 miles away. One man strapped on his skates and rolled into Washington, D.C., on that warm day, August 28, 1963. They all came to the Washington Monument just as the sun began its slow, hot dance across the sky.

They came to hear Martin and other civil rights leaders inspire ~~a nation~~.

They came because they believed that all people should be treated equally.

They came because they wanted to belong.

They came in search of one thing: Freedom.

# THEY CAME TO MARCH!

**M**artin traveled to Washington, D.C., the night before he was to give his speech. He had come from Atlanta, Georgia, where our family lived. He checked into the Willard Hotel so that he could prepare his speech in a quiet place, with no interruptions.

My brother worked very hard on his speeches. He understood how important each and every one of his words would be. He wrote them, and scratched them out, and wrote down some more. Martin practiced reading his speeches over and over again.

He stayed up all night in his hotel room. Not once did he stop to eat, or even lay his head down on his pillow for a quick nap. That was Martin. Even if he'd wanted to sleep, he couldn't—the words of his speech kept him awake. **HIS SPEECH WOULDN'T LET HIM REST.**

Martin was still writing when the sun came up. He was still making changes and corrections to his speech. The hours had passed quickly. The time was rushing ahead very fast. Afternoon was not far off. Soon it would be time to deliver his speech. My brother always liked putting the final touches on his words before he spoke them publicly. So he read his speech quietly to make sure it conveyed the message he wanted his listeners to hear.

Then Martin washed his face and changed into one of his best dark suits. Martin was a third-generation preacher. Our grandfather, the Reverend A. D. Williams, and our daddy, whose name also was Martin, had taught all of us King children many lessons about being an effective leader. They had told us to always be prepared with our best clothes when making public appearances. So, even though it was a hot summer day, Martin wore a clean starched shirt and a tie. He tucked his speech into his breast pocket. He was ready.

Martin met up with the organizers of the march, some of the most respected civil rights leaders of the day—James Farmer, John Lewis, A. Philip Randolph, Bayard Rustin, Roy Wilkins, and Whitney Young. Together, they headed over to the Capitol to talk to a delegation from Congress about passing a law that would have **BLACK PEOPLE TREATED THE SAME AS WHITE PEOPLE.**

**W**hile Martin met with the leaders, the marchers gathered at the foot of the Washington Monument, where they listened to great singers of the time sing freedom songs such as "Blowin' in the Wind" and **"WE SHALL OVERCOME."** This was how the march began.

Once most of the people had come together, they started to march toward the Lincoln Memorial, where the day's most electrifying speakers and entertainers were gathering. There were students and poor people. Christians walked arm in arm with Jewish people. **BLACK PEOPLE HELD HANDS WITH WHITE PEOPLE.** And even though they were from very different worlds, they were all marching for the same reason. Oh, was it a sight to see! I had been to many marches with my brother Martin, but it was clear from the beginning that this one was special.

Finally, someone rushed into the room where Martin and the other leaders were meeting. "Dr. King! Look out the window!"

Martin rubbed his eyes and peeked through the curtain. He could hardly believe what he saw. There was a blanket of people, walking shoulder to shoulder. They were all kinds of folks, looking like patches of color in a great quilt spread over the National Mall in Washington. There were thousands.

**CHANTING.**

**WANTING.**

**READY.**

**MARCHING!**

Martin rushed out onto the Capitol steps. He and the other leaders hurried down to the street to join the marchers. I always knew my brother was a powerful man, but when he and those other men walked together on that day, they were a mighty force. **THE SEA OF MARCHERS PARTED FOR MARTIN AND HIS FRIENDS.** The marchers opened up to welcome these men who were paving their way. The six leaders smiled as they began to blaze the road to equality.

Coretta, Martin's wife, who was always like a sister to me, was not far behind. Her heart swelled with pride. As Martin walked, he saw fathers carrying their children on their shoulders, waving and pointing, and saying, "That's Reverend Martin Luther King!" Grandmothers and grandfathers were dressed in their Sunday best, nodding and wishing Martin well. Their voices lifted praise into the heavens and filled the air with a joyful song: *"WOKE UP THIS MORNING WITH MY MIND STAYED ON FREEDOM! HALLELU, HALLELU, HALLELUJAH!"*

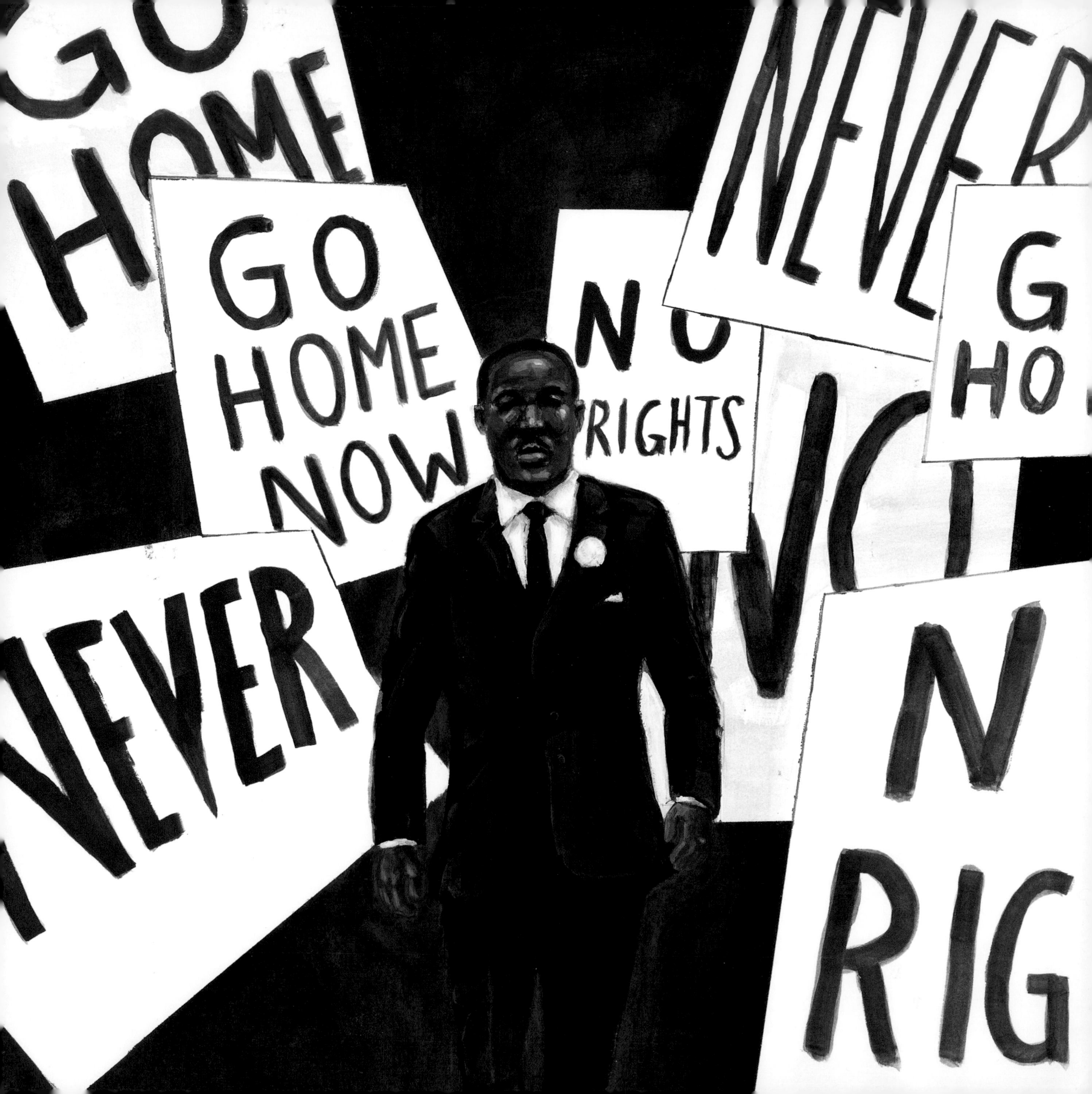
GO HOME
GO HOME NOW
NO RIGHTS
NEVER

Martin didn't pay much attention to the police and the armed guards who'd been sent from towns all over Maryland to keep order. And he wasn't worried, either, about the angry people who yelled and made mean faces and hurled hurtful words at him. Some people even hoped Martin and the marchers would be scared off, or that they'd get upset enough to say and do bad things back. They should have known this much: Martin didn't scare easily. And he and his marchers, who had always practiced nonviolence, came to Washington, D.C., **WITH LOVE IN THEIR HEARTS, NOT HATE.**

Peace is certainly what Martin had on his mind as he stood next to the marble statue of President Abraham Lincoln, where he spent most of the afternoon helping other speakers put the final touches on their speeches, and shaking hands with people who had come, too, to make their voices heard.

OME

O

HTS NEVER

As a preacher, my brother knew how to influence a crowd. He knew that one of the best ways to get folks to listen was to present them with a good singer. Even though the day had been full of people singing freedom songs and putting their beliefs to music, Martin was especially pleased when he saw that his friend, the legendary gospel singer Mahalia Jackson, had come to Washington on that day. Martin leaned toward Mahalia and whispered, "We need a song, Mahalia. Sing!"

And oh, did Mahalia sing. She let loose on the old slave spiritual "I've Been 'Buked, and I've Been Scorned." That song was slow and sad, but defiant. Just the kind of song Martin thought would help remind people why they had gathered together on that hot summer day.

Mahalia's magnificent alto rolled over the National Mall in Washington like soft thunder. *"I'm gonna tell my Lord, when I get home/Just how long they've been treating me wrong!"* she sang, teasing and stretching each one of those eloquent words.

The marchers were moved to shout.

## "SING, MAHALIA!"

## "TELL IT LIKE IT IS!"

When folks got to carrying on, Martin knew they were ready to receive his words. He stepped to the podium and looked out, taking in the precious sight of so many eager people staring back at him.

As soon as Martin began to speak, he found a rhythm that was all his own. There was no stopping my brother. Soon he wasn't even looking at the words he'd labored over the night before. His speech took on a force all its own. He spoke with clarity and conviction. His friend Mahalia shouted to him, "Tell them about your dream, Martin!" And he did. He used his words to paint a picture so vivid you could almost see the snowcapped mountains in Colorado, the slopes of California, the Stone Mountain of Georgia and even the molehills of Mississippi that he described in his speech. He spoke of people of all colors, from all nations, getting along—working together and praying together and standing up for freedom. **TOGETHER IN "A BEAUTIFUL SYMPHONY OF BROTHERHOOD," HE SAID.**

My brother Martin had a dream. He shared it with the marchers. He shared it with the nation. And the world. It was a beautiful, inspirational dream. One day, he said, children would live in a nation where they would be judged by the content of their character, not the color of their skin—where black boys and girls would be able to join hands with white boys and girls as sisters and brothers.

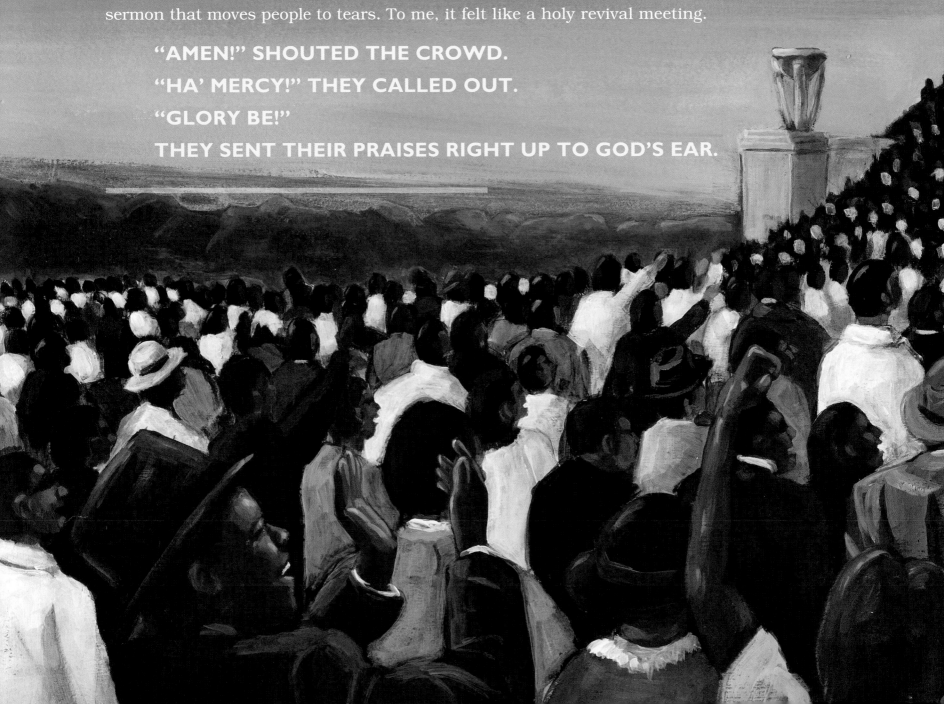

Martin's words were as loud as thunder. When he spoke, I could feel myself filling with pride. Not the "chesty"pride that Mother Dear and Daddy always warned us against, but the kind of pride that comes from seeing your very own brother touch so many people in such a big way. And I could see the legacy of our family of ministers coming through Martin. For so many years I'd watched Martin preach in a congregation, speaking from the pulpit. But today he was preaching to a nation. He was on fire. He was giving the kind of sermon that moves people to tears. To me, it felt like a holy revival meeting.

"AMEN!" SHOUTED THE CROWD.
"HA' MERCY!" THEY CALLED OUT.
"GLORY BE!"
THEY SENT THEIR PRAISES RIGHT UP TO GOD'S EAR.

My brother was making history. He was changing the world. And reminding everyone that we're all God's children, and all from a great nation that believes in liberty. And that is the only way for America to move forward. **"FREE AT LAST, FREE AT LAST, THANK GOD ALMIGHTY, WE'RE FREE AT LAST!"** Martin shouted. And that patchwork quilt of people, who had come from small towns and big cities, clapped and cheered and let their tears flow.

I couldn't hold in my excitement. I knew something special had just happened. I was clasping my hands to my heart, and smiling. I got chills listening to my brother speak.

Mother Dear and Daddy and Alfred Daniel and I knew that a change was surely going to come. Martin and his dream had inspired people to help make that change happen. There was so much hope in Martin's speech. Hope for all of us. Hope for the whole world.

On that day, my brother and all those who marched in Washington taught us all about **THE POWER OF WORDS,** and how important it is to work together and raise our voices, to speak up. **IT IS A DAY THAT WILL LAST IN THE HEARTS AND MEMORIES OF ALL AMERICANS**—that beautiful quilt of people, standing tall, taking a stand, and making a difference. For you. For me. For us all.

# AUTHOR'S NOTE

The year 1963 had been eye-opening. In April, my brother Martin was arrested and jailed for conducting voter registration drives; Governor George Wallace infamously prohibited two black students from integrating the University of Alabama; and television viewers all over the world saw African American demonstrators set upon by snarling dogs and powerful water hoses wielded by police officers. These events weighed heavily on the minds of the American people. So, in June of that year, when civil rights activist A. Philip Randolph announced there would soon be a massive protest, its relevance and importance was understood by many.

The March on Washington for Jobs and Freedom was one of the largest and most successful protests in our nation's history. On August 28, more than 250,000 marchers gathered on the National Mall, an impressive number, considering organizers had held their first planning meeting less than two months earlier. The "Big Six" was a name given to some of the most prominent civil rights leaders of that time: James Farmer, John Lewis, A. Philip Randolph, Bayard Rustin, Roy Wilkins, and Whitney Young.

These men outlined their demands for bringing equality to the nation: Congress's adoption of President John F. Kennedy's civil rights legislation; integration of all public schools by the end of the year; job training and placement for unemployed black Americans; and a law barring job discrimination against African Americans.

Charged with organizing the logistics of the march, Bayard Rustin had a budget of $120,000 to make arrangements. He raised even more money by selling march buttons and programs. The government was also making preparations. Motorcycle escorts, police officers, army troops, and even judges were armed, ready, and on guard. President Kennedy was so nervous that he tried to get my brother to use his influence and call off the event. Still, the march took place—and not one person was arrested or jailed on this historic day of nonviolent protest!

Many popular entertainers came to march that day—among them were Josephine Baker, Harry Belafonte, Marlon Brando, Sammy Davis, Jr., Charlton Heston, Lena Horne, Paul Newman, and Sidney Poitier. Dorothy Height, the president of the National Council of Negro Women, was on the speaker's platform when Martin gave his speech. Ms. Height was one of many female foot soldiers who contributed to the success of the march.

Unfortunately, I wasn't with Martin on that day. I thought it was important to stay home in Atlanta with our parents, who, by that time, would have been a little overwhelmed by the crowd and the daylong event. But my family and I watched the march on television, and our hearts were with Martin every step of the way. We could feel his words as if he were with us.

"I Have a Dream" went down in history as one of the greatest orations of modern times. Standing in front of the Lincoln Memorial—a statue dedicated to the man who had written the Emancipation Proclamation one hundred years earlier—my brother spoke for freedom. And while he inspired the nation to help itself, he himself drew strength from this incredible tide of people, marching arm in arm, to make the world a better place.

—CHRISTINE KING FARRIS